IF I WERE A DRAGON

**Mariana Books
Rhyming Series
Book 7
Imagination**

By
Roger Carlson
Illustrated by Chaudhary Gohar

Liam was a boy with a vivid imagination.
He loved imagining creatures beyond earth's creation.

1

At the end of the day,
when he lay on his bed,
thoughts about dragons
started filling his head.

Could I be a dragon instead of a boy?
Would I be too big for my favorite toy?

I wonder what kind of dragon I would be?
If I was a dragon, would I still be me?

Would I be a baby dragon,
still growing my wings?
Begging my daddy dragon for
all the little things!

Would I have a big head
that bumped into trees?
Would I make a tornado
when I had to sneeze?

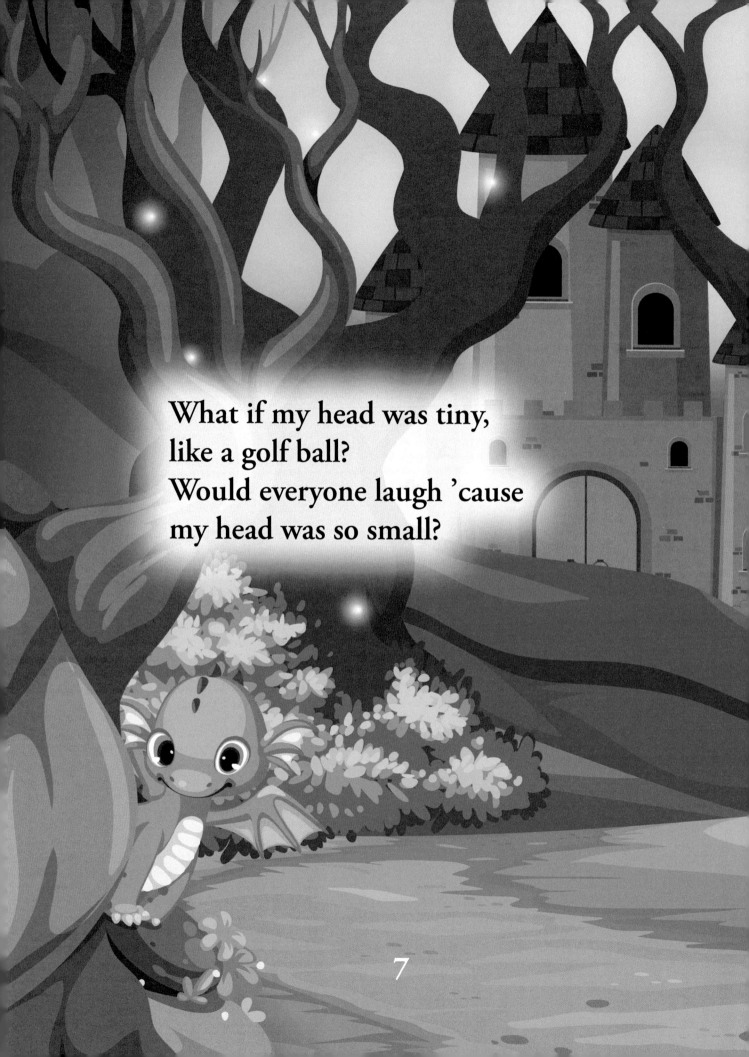

What if my head was tiny,
like a golf ball?
Would everyone laugh 'cause
my head was so small?

Would I have a big tail to shoo away the flies? I'd swish it and pests would take off for the skies.

Or would I have a small tail
to help me move quick?
I'd wag it and use it to do a
cool trick!

If I was a dragon, what color would I be?
Would my scaly skin be dark blue like the sea?

Or would I be brown, like
the mud under foot?
Or black like a fireplace
covered in soot?

11

Would I be green with an emerald glow?
A rich green like a summer meadow.

Or would I be as red as
a sweet candy cane?
Could I fly in the air
like a big airplane?

Would I have giant teeth to chew all my food?
I wonder what a dragon's menu would include!

14

What if I had small teeth
like those of a rat?
I'd spend all day chewing
food, but I'd never get fat!

Would I have huge claws like a big grizzly bear?
I'd use them to catch prey and then to comb my long hair!

16

Or would I have small nails
to cling on to my fruits?
To dig out all the carrots
and all the fennel roots?

Would I be a dragon who
breathes scary red fire?
I could fly through the sky
and look oh so dire!

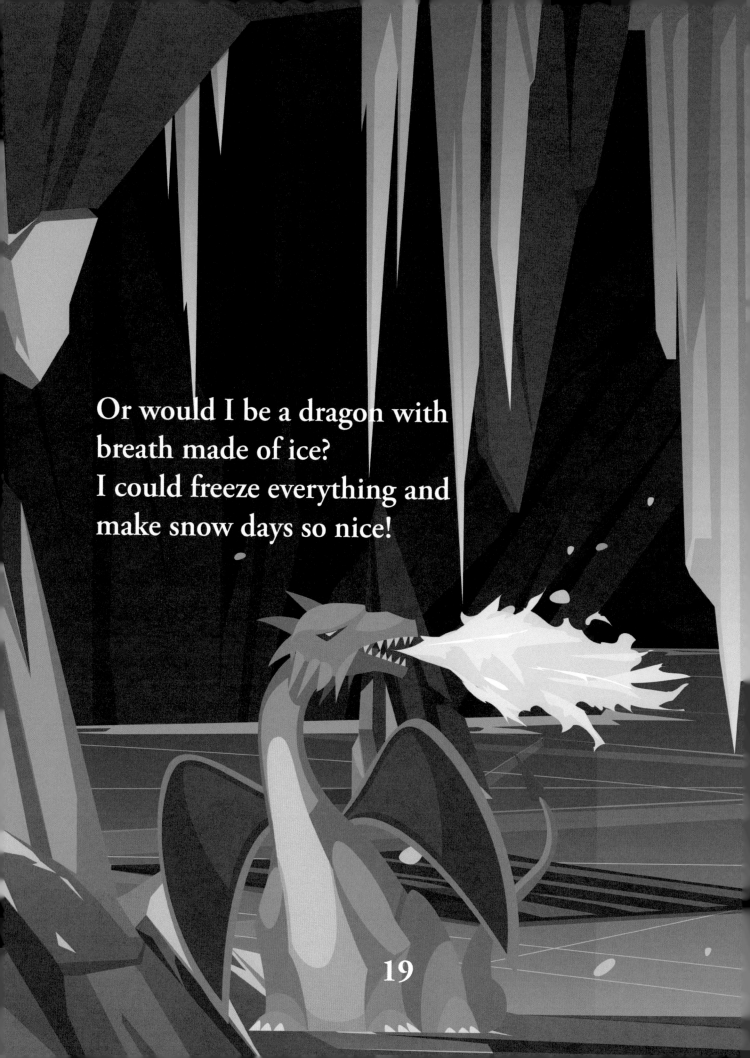

Or would I be a dragon with
breath made of ice?
I could freeze everything and
make snow days so nice!

19

Or would I breathe smoke, my breath shady and black?
I'd burp clouds of smoke after my daily snack!

20

Would I live under water, like a huge fish?
I'd swim in the ocean, wherever I wish!

Where would I settle if I lived on land? Would I make my home in the trees or on the sand?

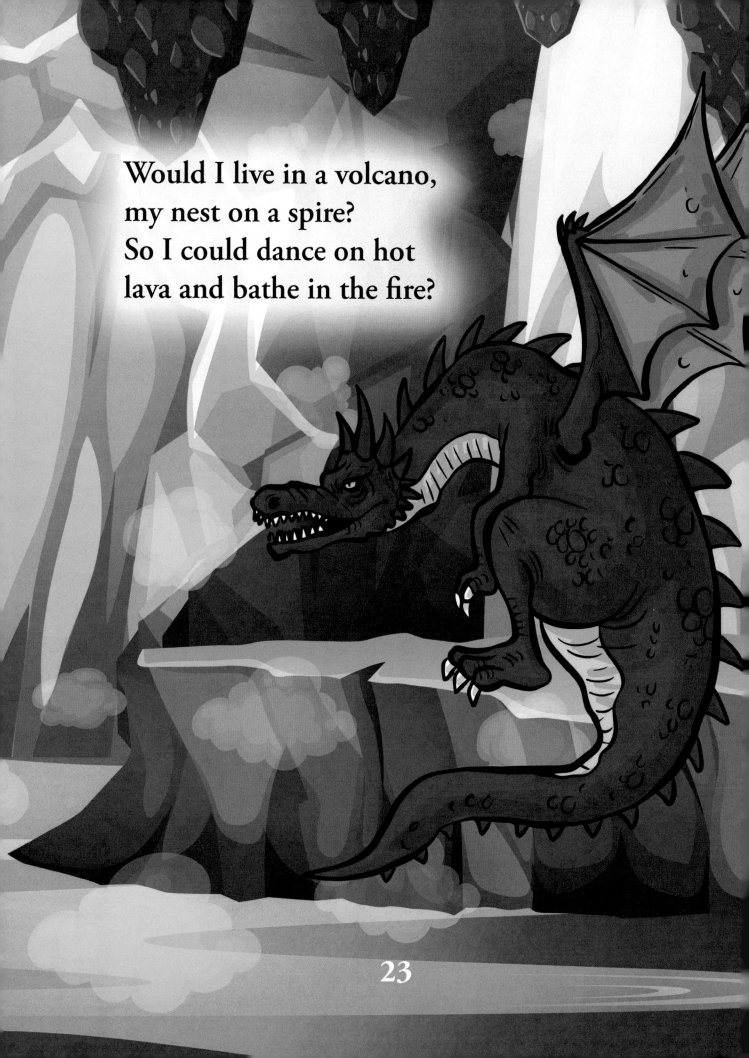

Would I live in a volcano,
my nest on a spire?
So I could dance on hot
lava and bathe in the fire?

Could I live on an ice planet covered in snow? I'd eat ice cream all day and sled down the ice floe!

Maybe I'd live on a desert planet called "Barren Beast."
Where its sun would rise in the west and set in the east!

25

Would I be a nice dragon?
Would I show friends I care?
If a friend needed food,
would I happily share?

26

What if I was a mean dragon
who acted rude and fake?
If instead of sharing, I ate every
bite of steak?

27

Wait! Now I know what kind
of dragon I would be!
I'd be the best dragon of all:
I'd be me!

28

Right at this moment,
Mom and Dad came in,
Liam came back to reality
and sat up with a grin!

They kissed him goodnight and
tucked him up in bed.
He drifted off to sleep with a
dream in his head.

He dreamt about dragons
all through the night,
Best little dragon, Liam
would surely sleep tight!

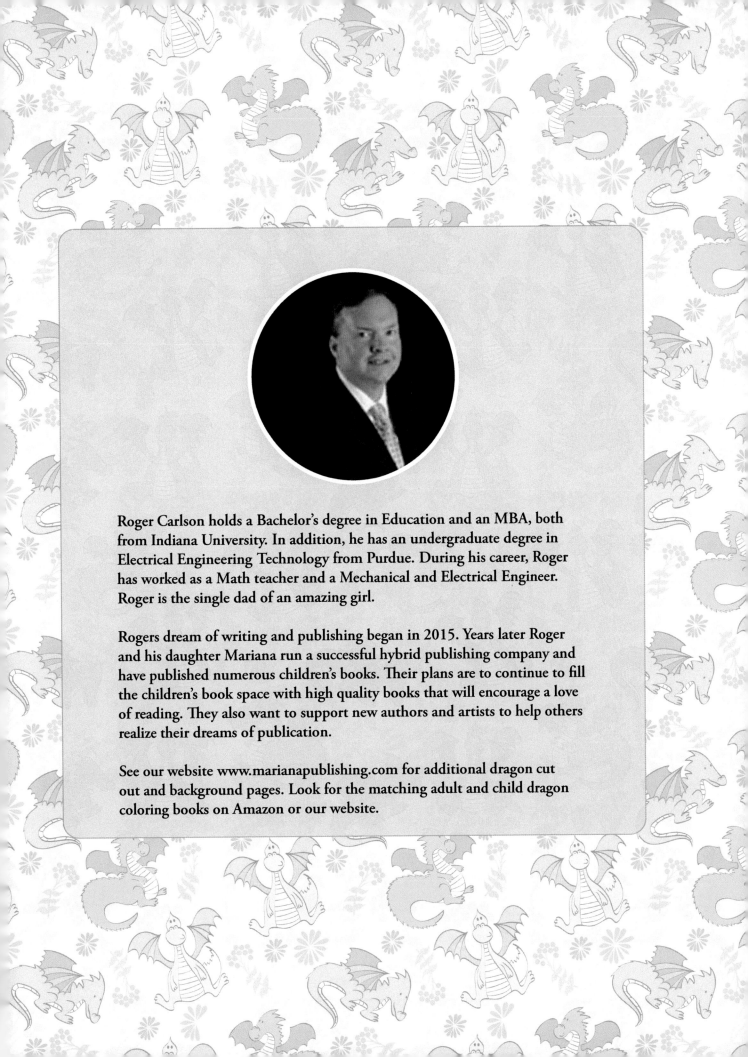

Roger Carlson holds a Bachelor's degree in Education and an MBA, both from Indiana University. In addition, he has an undergraduate degree in Electrical Engineering Technology from Purdue. During his career, Roger has worked as a Math teacher and a Mechanical and Electrical Engineer. Roger is the single dad of an amazing girl.

Rogers dream of writing and publishing began in 2015. Years later Roger and his daughter Mariana run a successful hybrid publishing company and have published numerous children's books. Their plans are to continue to fill the children's book space with high quality books that will encourage a love of reading. They also want to support new authors and artists to help others realize their dreams of publication.

See our website www.marianapublishing.com for additional dragon cut out and background pages. Look for the matching adult and child dragon coloring books on Amazon or our website.

WAYBACK BOOKS

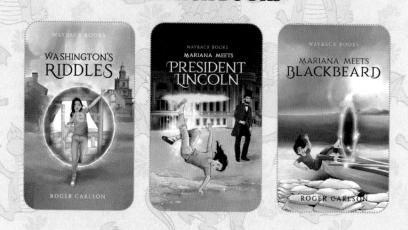

Find us on:

Copyright © 2021 by Roger Carlson

ISBN: 978-1-64510-058-4 (Hardback)
ISBN: 978-1-64510-057-7 (Amazon Paperback)
ISBN: 978-1-64510-059-1 (Print On Demand)
ISBN: 978-1-64510-066-9 (Hardback Print on Demand)

Build your own dragon cut outs

Feel free to copy these pages and reuse over and over.

Project Example

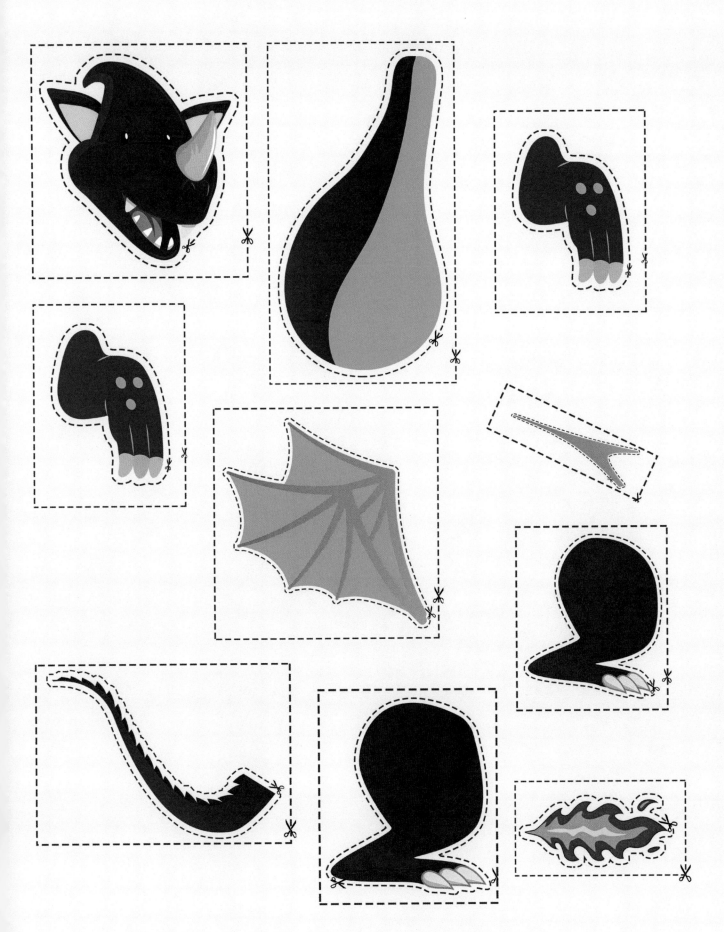

Made in the USA
Middletown, DE
20 June 2022

67356558R00024